John Malvin

Autobiography of John Malvin

A Narrative, Containing an Authentic Account of his Fifty Years Struggle in

the State of Ohio

John Malvin

Autobiography of John Malvin
A Narrative, Containing an Authentic Account of his Fifty Years Struggle in the State of Ohio

ISBN/EAN: 9783744673297

Printed in Europe, USA, Canada, Australia, Japan

Cover: Foto ©Raphael Reischuk / pixelio.de

More available books at **www.hansebooks.com**

AUTOBIOGRAPHY

OF

JOHN MALVIN.

A NARRATIVE,

CONTAINING AN AUTHENTIC ACCOUNT OF HIS FIFTY YEARS' STRUGGLE
IN THE STATE OF OHIO IN BEHALF OF THE AMERICAN SLAVE, AND
THE EQUAL RIGHTS OF ALL MEN BEFORE THE LAW WITHOUT
REFERENCE TO RACE OR COLOR; FORTY-SEVEN YEARS
OF SAID TIME BEING EXPENDED IN THE
CITY OF CLEVELAND.

———

CLEVELAND :
LEADER PRINTING COMPANY, 146 SUPERIOR STREET.
1879.

PREFACE.

Many of my friends of this city desiring me to give to the public the history of my life, and the details and incidents connected therewith, I hesitated for a long time to make the undertaking, but from their continual solicitations, I at last concluded to write a narrative, which, strictly speaking, is no history of my life, but an enumeration of the principal events which have occurred, and with which I have been personally connected. Not having a record to guide me, I have been obliged to rely entirely on my memory. It is very possible, therefore, that there may be some slight errors as to dates, and matters of minor importance, but as to the events themselves, I can safely assure my friends that they are related substantially as they occurred.

AUTOBIOGRAPHY

CHAPTER I.

I was born in Prince William County, Virginia, in the year 1795, in a little town known by the name of Dumfries. My mother, whose name was Daleus Malvin, was a free woman, but my father was a slave belonging to a man named Henderson. In my seventh year I was bound out to this Henderson as an apprentice. Henderson also lived in Dumfries, owned several farms in Wood County, W. Va., and was a large slave owner. He had a clerk named John Griffith, who was an unmarried man, and whose business it was to keep the accounts of the several farms, and I was assigned by Mr. Henderson to wait upon this clerk. I attended him personally, blacked his boots, took care of his horse, and so on, and when through with these avocations, at times, I would go out into the field and work with the other hands. At dinner time my duty was to go to the house and prepare the table. After dinner I would return again to the field. Such was my daily employment.

I was kept regularly at this employment for nearly four years, when, in the year 1807, the people of Wood County were greatly agitated and aroused by the discovery of a plotted rebellion, which had been fomented by Dominick Blennerhassett and Aaron Burr, who had their headquarters at Blennerhassett Island, on the

Ohio River, three miles below the mouth of the Little Kanawha. I was at that time removed from my present situation to one of the farms in that vicinity, situated on what is known as Cow Creek, and remained there until the breaking out of the war of 1812. Griffith had preceded me to this farm, and when I arrived there I was kept at substantially the same occupation. During this period I had a fair opportunity of witnessing the miseries of slavery. Though I was an apprentice, I was treated little better than a slave myself. For my clothing, I was supplied every year with one pair of shoes, two pairs of tow linen pantaloons, one pair of negro cotton pantaloons, and a negro cotton round jacket. My food consisted of one peck of corn meal a week. Sometimes I received a supply of salt, but they were very sparing of that luxury, and I was compelled most of the time to go without it. I was obliged to resort to other means to obtain food.

The luxury which I observed among the neighboring slave-owners, and the style of living of my master, stimulated my appetite for some of the good things of this world, and being of an adventurous spirit, like most other boys, I concluded to avail myself of any means that would enable me to procure something more substantial than corn meal. There was another boy on the farm who was a little older than myself, and who roomed with me in the same cabin. Whenever we felt a desire for meat we would provide ourselves with clubs, and in the night time visit the hog beds. The hogs were allowed to run at large in the woods, and when we would find a sow with her pigs, we would drive her up and make a selection of one of the pigs, and by good use of our clubs secure the fruit of our adventure. We would then take the pig to our cabin, make a hot fire, and, instead of scalding, we would singe the hair off from the pig. . Then we would dress and roast the pig to our fancy, which, with our corn bread, made us a meal which we relished all the more by reason of the risk and danger we ran in obtaining it. When we wanted a change in our diet we would go out among the cows and get some milk. In our first adventure of this kind I procured a jug; I inserted the teat into the mouth of the jug and was about to proceed milking, when the cow made a sudden movement with one of her hind legs and struck me on the thigh. I fell over and lay until the pain subsided, when I got up and found another cow more docile than the first, and succeeded in getting the jug filled. Roast pig was well enough in its way, but we sometimes wanted a change of meat, and then we would go out among the sheep and catch a lamb, and unbutton its collar (cut its throat.)

One night I had retired as usual, to sleep, but before retiring I had placed a pot of water over the fire place, in which I had put my shirt to boil. When I woke up I found to my dismay that the pot was glowing red, and that all the water had boiled out. At the bottom of the pot was a hand full of ashes, being all that remained of my shirt. This was the only shirt I had, and when I notified the clerk of my mishap, in order to recompense me for my loss, he gave me a severe flogging, and through the whole winter I was obliged to go without a shirt on my back and no covering but my jacket.

On the breaking out of the war of 1812 I attempted to run away, and for that purpose I followed a body of soldiers. I attempted to get aboard one of their boats on the Ohio River, but not succeeding, I was compelled to return to my station, and I never was missed, nor was the fact of my leaving ever discovered.

On another occasion I was taken by this clerk Griffith, my wrists were tied crosswise together, and my hands were then brought down and tied to my ankles; my shirt was taken off, and in that condition I was compelled to lie on the ground, and he began flogging me. He whipped me on one side till the flesh was all raw and bleeding; then he rolled me over like a log and whipped me on the other side in the same manner. When I was untied I put on my shirt. So severely was my flesh lacerated that my shirt stuck to my back, and I was unable to get it off without the assistance of an old lady who lived on the farm, who applied grease to it. I had committed no crime or offense that justified any such treatment. He had ordered me to chop some logs, so that they could be rolled together to be burned. His brother was to attend to the burning of the logs, and I had chopped them and went away. The logs had been rolled together and a fire started, but by some accident the fire reached the fence and burnt five or six of the panels. As soon as I heard of this I ran to the fence and stopped the fire from spreading, and sat there until 12 o'clock at night to watch and keep the cattle from going through into the corn. The clerk then came home, and finding things in this condition, he stripped and whipped me in the manner I have stated. I resolved at that time that if ever I should grow older and stronger I would kill him, but I never got an opportunity to be revenged upon him, as in 1813 Mr. Henderson died, and I was at liberty again, and returned to my parents in East Virginia, and never saw the clerk afterwards.

My father was a carpenter by trade, and I began to work with him at his bench until I had learned the trade. During the time I was working with my father I became possessed of a desire to learn to read. When

I would see people read a newspaper or book. I felt great delight in what seemed to me to be *pretty talking*, as I considered it. When I heard any one read, my curiosity would be excited, and I would listen attentively to the matter read, and I at last concluded that I should like to *talk pretty* too, like the white people. An excellent opportunity was afforded me. I knew an old slave who was past labor, and who lived in a cabin three miles from where I did, and who by some means had learned to read. He could read the Bible quite readily, and he consented to teach me to read and spell. We obtained light to read by means of pine knots, which I would go out and find in the dark by feeling with my feet. I would carry them to the old man's cabin and put them in the fire-place. We did not dare to talk loud, lest we should be overheard, and had to confine ourselves to whispers. Such were the means and circumstances under which I learned to read and spell. After I had learned to read I began to attend several religious meetings, and became so wrought up with religious fervor that I concluded to preach the gospel. I joined the Baptist Church, and, though I had no education, I applied to the church of which I was a member, for a license to preach. That not being permissible under the laws of Virginia, by reason of my color, the church refused to give me a license, but gave me a verbal permission to preach the gospel.

I began preaching among the slaves, and even solemnized marriages by permission from the owners. While preaching, I continued to live with my parents, and remained with them until 1827, during which time I availed myself of every opportunity I could get, to read, whenever I could obtain a paper or book. Nothing eventful occurred to me, however, during this period, until I left my home, as I shall relate in the following chapter.

CHAPTER II.

In the year 1827, a spirit of adventure, natural to most young men, took possession of me, and I concluded to leave Virginia and go to Ohio. No colored man was permitted to travel through Virginia without producing evidences in some way of his freedom. I had a short time prior to my departure, applied for and obtained freedom papers, to which was affixed the signature of the Clerk of the County, and the seal of the Court.

I affectionately took leave of my parents, with nothing but my clothes that were on my back, and an extra shirt, and started a foot on my journey, by way of what was called the Winchester Road. The first village I came to after crossing Cedar Run, was Brentsville; the second was Hay Market, passing the Bull Run Mountain at what was called the Thoroughfare Gap; then pursuing my course until I came to Oak Hill, the residence of Chief Justice Marshall; then crossing the Blue Ridge Mountain at Ashly's Gap, then down along the Shenandoah River, crossing that at Berry's Ferry, leaving Millwood and Whitepost to the left; thence to Winchester, Frederick County; thence crossing the south branch of the Potomac, near Rumley's and so on to Cheat River and Patterson Creek. At Rumley I stopped at a magistrates office and produced the necessary papers of my freedom, and was permitted to proceed. That was the only magistrate I called on during my journey. Shortly after leaving Rumley, I was met by two men, one of whom had a dog and rifle. They asked me who I was, and demanded proof. I showed them my papers, and they let me pass.

I forded all the streams mentioned, and then came to Clarksburg, the metropolis of Harrison County, thence to the Dry Ridge in Wood County, and from thence to the Ohio River, to the farm where I had formerly lived on Cow Creek ; crossing Cow Creek, Calf Creek and Bull Creek and so on down the river, until I came opposite Marietta, and there I crossed by ferry. The boy who was rowing me over the river, had got to the middle of the stream, when he was discovered by his employer, who, seeing that I was a colored man, ordered the boy to row me back. He then asked me some questions, and I presented my freedom papers, and, after examining them he allowed the boy to row me across. I walked a distance of 300 miles, from Prince William County to Marietta, Ohio, in the short space of six days.

At Marietta, I got aboard of a flat boat on the Ohio River, and worked my passage to Cincinnati, which was then a growing town. I thought upon coming to a free State like Ohio, that I would find every door thrown open to receive me, but from the treatment I received by the people generally, I found it little better than in Virginia.

I had not been long in Cincinnati, before I became acquainted with many of the colored people there residing, and it was there I first began to interest myself in the condition of my race. My attention had been called to a statute of Ohio, in which I read substantially these words: "That no negro or mulatto should be permitted " to emigrate to this State, or settle, or acquire a domi- " cile, without first entering into bonds of $500, with ap- " proved security, conditioned that he would never be- " come a town charge, and that he would keep the " peace." I read on a little further : "That no negro " or mulatto shall testify in a Court of Justice or Record, " where a party in a cause there pending was white. No

" negro or mulatto child shall enter into any of the pub-
" lic schools of this State, or receive the benefit of the
" school fund. No negro or mulatto shall be permitted
" to enter any of the institutions of this State, viz: a
" lunatic asylum, deaf and dumb asylum, nor even the
" poor house."

Thus I found every door closed against the colored
man in a free State, excepting the jails and penitentia-
ries, the doors of which were thrown wide open to receive him. I was for some time uncertain whether to
remain in Ohio, or to return to Virginia, but at length
concluded to remain in Ohio for a time, not knowing
what to do. I succeeded in calling together a meeting
of the colored men of Cincinnati, and, on consultation,
things did not look very encouraging. I suggested to
the meeting the propriety of appointing a committee to
go to some country with power to make arrangements
for the purchase of some place to live free from the
trammels of unsocial and unequal laws.

None but those who have experienced the misery of
servitude, or the pangs which result form the conscious-
ness of being despised as a caste, from being shut out
from the benefit of enjoying the pure atmosphere of
heaven in common with all mankind, and not only
being personally despised, but not even having the protection of the laws themselves, can fully appreciate the
patriotic ardor which animated that little assembly.
That we should find a home that we could consider
wholly our own, where we could all be on an equal
social footing, warmed us up to an unusual degree of
enthusiasm. A committee consisting of James King,
Henry Archer and Israel Lewis, was appointed for that
purpose. The committee went to Canada, and entered
into negotiations with a Canadian Land Company, for
30,000 acres of land, located on the Sabel River, to

form a colony. The colony was soon afterwards formed, and took the name of Wilberforce, after the great anti-slavery champion.

During the time that the committee was absent, I called a meeting of the colored men of Cincinnati, for the purpose of petitioning the Legislature for the repeal of those obnoxious black laws. We drew up a petition to which we obtained numerous signatures, and among others, those of Nicholas Longworth, Wykoff Piatt and John Klingman. This petition, after it had been put in circulation, raised a great deal of comment. We saw published in one of the daily papers of Cincinnati, the following notice from members of one of the colored churches:

"We, the undersigned, members of the Methodist "Episcopal Church, 200 in number, do certify that we "form no part of that indefinite number that are asking "a change in the laws of Ohio; all we ask, is a continu- "ation of the smiles of the white people as we have "hitherto enjoyed them." Signed,

ABRAHAM DANGERFIELD.
JACK HARRIS.
THOMAS ARNOLD.
GEORGE JONES.
JOSEPH KITE.

There were at this time two colored Methodist Churches in Cincinnati—the African M. E. Church, and the M. E. Church,—the latter being the publishers of the above article. The former church was in favor of the repeal of those obnoxious laws, and we continued the circulation of our petition until we got it numerously signed and sent it to the legislature. What became of our petition, or what action the legislature took in the matter, we never found out, but from the position taken by some of our colored brethren, it is likely that the legislature thought best not to interfere in the matter.

During my residence in Cincinnati, I was frequently in the habit of visiting the boats and steamers on the Ohio River, as I was fond of looking at them, especially the machinery. On one of these occasions I visited two boats, and then a third boat which was called the "Criterion." The boats lay close to each other, and on board of the "Criterion" there were thirty slaves bound for the southern market. I was standing on the permanent deck of the "Criterion" when a woman of interesting appearance passed near me, coming from the hurricane deck. I spoke to her and found her name to be Susan Hall, and that she was from the same county where I was born. I had never seen her before, but my mother had often seen her, and spoken of her to me. She told me that she had two children aboard, a boy and a girl. I asked her if she would like to be free. She said she would like it very much. I had to leave off talking with her then, as the watch was very strict, and told her I had to go over into Kentucky, but would return that same night. So great was my abhorrence of slavery, that I was willing to run any risk to accomplish the liberation of a slave. I crossed over into Kentucky, and returned between sundown and dark, and went aboard of the boat. There I remained until about one o'clock, when the woman made her appearance with one of her children. She told me that things were so situated that she could not get her girl without discovery, and we were obliged to leave without the girl. There were two gangways on the boat; one forward and one aft. The gang-plank at the stern was drawn in, and there was no means of exit from the boat except by the forward gang plank. It was impossible, however, for us to escape at that place, as

two men were posted there with guns as watch. On
looking around, however, I found there was a small
boat belonging to the "Criterion," in the water at the
stern. I concluded to make use of this boat for the
purpose of effecting the escape. I assisted the woman
and her boy into the little boat and untied it from the
"Criterion." There was another large steamer astern
of the "Criterion," and I shot the little boat quickly
out under the bow of this other steamer, and made it
appear as though I was leaving that steamer instead of
the "Criterion." The guards were deluded by this
ruse, and paid no attention to us, thinking we came
from the other boat. The risk, however, was very
great. We could see the barrels of their guns glisten
in the moonlight. I effected a landing and brought
them to a place of safety. Then I returned and succeeded in getting aboard of the "Criterion" again, and
in the same manner I succeeded in effecting the escape
of two young men and a young woman.

I found shelter in a safe place in Cincinnati for the
woman and child; the others I sent with a guide, to
Richmond, Indiana. The woman was pregnant, and
remained in Cincinnati till she was in a condition
to travel, during which time I paid for her board and
sustenance. I then sent her to Canada, where she married a man named McKinney, and raised a family.
One of her sons has often been seen on the streets of
Cleveland. His name is Courtney McKinney, and he is
a chimney-sweep. He wears on his cap a plate with
his name and occupation engraved thereon.

At the time when I effected the escape of the slaves,
they were not missed until the next morning, and when
they were found to be missing the city was thrown into
great commotion, and constables were sent in all direc-
tions to search for the missing slaves; but they did not
succeed in finding them, nor was I ever suspected.

CHAPTER III.

On the 8th day of March, 1829, I married my present wife in Cincinnati, and the next August I moved to Louisville, Ky., and spent the remainder of the year at that place working at my trade. From there I moved shortly after to Middletown, nine miles from Louisville, and worked the next year there at my trade for one Chambers, the master of my wife's father, who was a slave. In the fall of the same year I was arrested as a fugitive slave and put in jail. The jailor procured sufficient aid to handcuff me, and tried to get a confession from me, having taken off my clothes, while he stood by with a cowhide in his hand in order to frighten and intimidate me, but he did not succeed in getting a confession from me, and he did not whip me either. I managed to procure bail for my appearance in Court at the March term, in the sum of $300, but on failure to prove that I was a slave, I was released from custody by the Court. The next April I left Louisville for the purpose of seeking a home for myself and wife in Canada, leaving my wife in Louisville. When I arrived in Canada I contracted for a small farm, and in the fall of the same year (1831) I returned to Louisville for my wife. In returning from Canada I procured passage aboard of a schooner at Buffalo, and proceeded up the lake, and a storm coming on we were forced to make harbor at Erie, and I concluded not to go by way of Cleveland, as I had first intended, for I thought the vessel was unsafe, but concluded to go by way of Pittsburgh. I started from Erie, and proceeded on foot fourteen miles to a little town called Waterford, in Pennsylvania. At

Waterford I purchased some scantling, and built me a small boat 4x18. I launched the boat into a stream at Waterford called Leboef Creek. I went down the creek in my little boat, and out of that creek into another creek, and pursued my way down that second stream until I came to French Creek, and there were a number of mills on French Creek, and dams were built across from one side to the other, and at some of those dams there were shutes, so that boats could pass through. Where there were no shutes I had to draw my boat out of the water, and drag it to places below the dam. There were great hills on both sides of French Creek, and the growth of the timber, which was principally hemlock, was very thick, and in the daytime it was so dark I could scarcely see my way through.

While proceeding down French Creek I was quite amused to see the Indians gathering the crude petroleum which was floating on top of the water. They gathered the oil by spreading blankets over the surface of the water, and allowing them to soak up the oil, and then they would take the blankets, and wring the oil out into vessels which they procured for that purpose. What they did with the oil I do not know.

Proceeding on, I arrived at the mouth of French Creek to a small town, (the name of which I have forgotten,) and from thence into the Allegheny River and down to Pittsburgh. I disposed of my boat at Pittsburgh, and with the proceeds I paid my passage to Cincinnati. My wife met me in Cincinnati, and then we started up the Ohio River as far as Portsmouth, Ohio, with what little household goods we had. My object was to reach Chillicothe, to which point the Ohio Canal had been completed, and then travel by way of the canal. I hired a team to take us and our goods to Chilli-

cothe, and from there we traveled on the canal to Newark, in Licking county. By this time cold weather had
set in, and we were compelled to spend the winter in
Newark.

In the following April, the canal being again open,
we proceeded on our journey, and arrived in Cleveland
the same month. There was very little communication
between the United States and Canada in those days,
so we waited in Cleveland for a good opportunity to
cross over into Canada, and finding no opportunity in
Cleveland we went to Buffalo, where we stayed a
few days. Here my wife became greatly troubled in
consequence of having left her father, and it lay so
heavily upon her that she gave me no rest. Seeing her
unwillingness to go to Canada, and her fears that she
would never see her father again, I concluded to give
up the farm, and my wife having taken a fancy to
Cleveland, we determined to go back and settle there.
We accordingly came to Cleveland, and I sought employment at my trade. But my color was an obstacle
and I could not get work of that kind. I managed,
however, to obtain employment as cook on the schooner
Aurora, that sailed on the lakes between Mackinaw and
Buffalo, and I kept that position for three months.
Leonard Case, Sr., and P. B. Andrews, of Cleveland,
had built a steam mill at the same spot where the C. &
P. R. R. shops now stand, and Mr. J. H. Hudson, who
was part owner of the vessel on which I was employed,
purchased that mill from Case and Andrews. The mill
was operated during the day, and he wanted to run it
also during the night. Mr. Hudson applied to me to act
as engineer during part of the time. A man by the name
of Erastus Smith and his son Washington were running
running the engine at the time. I was perfectly ignorant
of running an engine, and had no knowledge of machin-

ery, nor of steam power, and Mr. Hudson requested Mr.
Erastus Smith to instruct me how to run the engine. On
the day appointed at 12 o'clock I took charge of the engine.
Mr. Smith and his son that same day took their guns and
went out in the woods to hunt. They were gone nearly
two hours, and when they returned I heard Washington
ask his father some question which I did not compre-
hend, but the answer I understood very well. The
engine was running at a very rapid rate, and the blue
streaks of steam were passing through the joints of the
boiler. Mr. Smith answered, "I don't care if he blows
her to h—." I immediately sprang to the safety valve,
opened it, and let the steam blow off, for from his answer
I knew there was something wrong; then I left immediately and came to town, and I reported what had
occurred to P. B. Andrews, the gentleman who had
built the engine. He sent an engineer down to the mill
to see into the matter, and, on examination, he found
that there was only four inches of water in the boilers,
and that the supply cock was shut off, so that no water
could get into the boilers at all. I did not know how
the boilers were supplied with water. Mr. Smith or his
son must have shut it off before they went to the woods.
The engineer instructed me how to supply the boilers,
and we got things all right and started again. After
this the mill was only run during the day, and at night
I would take a portion of the engine apart, lay each
piece separate from the other, so that I would make no
mistake, and, in like manner, repeat my work at different times until I had taken the whole engine apart and
put it together again, and I became complete master of
the machinery.

I ran that engine twelve or thirteen months, and then
I communicated to Mr. Hudson a project I had formed
of buying my father-in-law's freedom. I opened cor-

respondence with his master, and he replied that he would take $400.00 for the old man, who was then sixty years of age, and that he would take $100.00 down, and the balance on time. I got a subscription paper and circulated it, and upon that subscription paper the public kindly donated $100.00. I then made two notes, payable in one and two years, for $150.00 each, and procured the endorsement thereon of John M. Sterling, Sr., Deacon Benjamin Rouse, Judith Richmond, and Thomas Whelpley. I sent my wife to Kentucky with the money and notes, and on paying the $100.00 and delivering the notes, her father was released, and came with her to Cleveland.

Hon. Samuel Williamson was the attorney for my father-in-law's master, and the notes, as they became due, were sent to Mr. Williamson for collection. Not being able to pay the first note, I was sued in the County Court. I expostulated with Mr. Williamson, and tried to be released from the obligation, to some extent at least. He replied to me, that though he was opposed to slavery, yet when a person agreed to pay money, it was morally wrong to refuse to do it. Judgment was rendered against me on the note, and I continued to work until I paid the notes.

My wife's father, whose name was Caleb Dorsey, lived in Cleveland fifteen years after his freedom was obtained, when, becoming anxious to visit his children in Louisville, he so informed my wife. We both protested against his going, as we thought the old man would not be able to chance the journey. Notwithstanding our entreaties, he persisted in going. He left Cleveland on a Friday, arriving in Louisville on Saturday night. The next day being Sabbath, he went to Church. On that same night he took the cholera, and died, at the age of seventy-five years.

During the first years of my residence in Cleveland, and while I was in the employ of Mr. Hudson, there was a little brick building on Academy Lane, owned by one Mr. Brewster, and which he allowed the congrega tion of the First Baptist Church, then organized, to use as a place of meeting and worship. I had, while in Cincinnati, obtained a license to preach the Gospel, from the Enon Baptist Church, and when I came to Cleveland, I occasionally preached for the First Baptist Church in the building on Academy Lane. I often received invitations to preach in the country, sometimes at Rockport, sometimes at Euclid, and other towns. My wife and myself have remained members of the Baptist Church ever since we were in Cleveland, and are still members thereof.

CHAPTER IV.

The extremity to which I had been driven, to pay the notes which I had given for the freedom of my wife's father, obliged me to resort to some means of earning the money to pay them. My earnings while in Mr. Hudson's employ, were barely sufficient to support my family. Through the kindness of Mr. James S. Clark, I was enabled to purchase, on easy terms, a vessel owned by Abraham Wright of Rockport. When I went to take out a license, the deputy Collector refused to grant it, deciding that my color was an obstacle. But when the Collector himself arrived, who was the Hon. Samuel Starkweather, well known to all the citizens of Cleveland, he decided that I had as much right to own and sail a vessel upon the lakes as I had to own a horse and buggy and drive through the streets, and he granted me a license. My vessel was called "The Grampus." After I obtained my license, Mr. Diodate Clark employed me to carry limestone and cedar posts from Kelley's and surrounding islands. I earned money enough to pay up the notes. I then disposed of the vessel.

My next employment was on the First Baptist Church, then on the corner of Champlain and Seneca streets, the place now occupied by the U. S. Organ Company. When the church was built and ready for dedication, the question was raised among the members as to where the colored people should sit. There was a diversity of opinion on the subject. In the first place, it was proposed to finish off the pews in the gallery in the same style as in the auditorium, and that I should have the finishing of it under my control and management; but finding that too expensive, they abandoned the method, and it was next proposed to the colored members that before the sale of the pews took place, that I, and one Stephen Griffin might make a selection of half a dozen pews anywhere in the church that might be suitable, whether on the broad or side aisle, or in front of the pulpit. To that I objected, stating that if I had to be colonized, I preferred to be colonized at Liberia, rather than in the House of God; that Christ or the Apostles never made any distinction on account of race or color. It was, however, decided that the colored people should sit in the gallery. On every proper occasion thereafter at church meetings I would bring up the question of the distinction of color in the house of worship, and the members became nearly divided on the question, and after struggling for eighteen months, it was finally concluded that the colored people should have the privilege of obtaining pews in any part of the building, as other persons, and my object was thus accomplished.

CHAPTER V.

During the year 1839 I was employed as a hand on the steamboat "Rochester," plying between Buffalo and Chicago. The following year I left this position, and purchased a canal boat from S. R. Hutchinson & Co. This firm owned the stone mill on the canal in Cleveland. My boat, which was called the "Auburn," was engaged in conveying wheat and merchandise on the Ohio Canal. The boat was a good passenger packet, with good cabins, and her former owners concluded to buy the boat back, which they did. They then employed me as captain, to manage her. On one occasion, while I was running the boat, after having loaded with merchandise, I was ordered to deliver the goods at Chillicothe. Leaving Cleveland about noon, we arrived at Niles about nine o'clock in the evening. At this place we were hailed by some person saying that a passenger wanted to get aboard to go south. We came alongside the dock and landed. Pretty soon after some baggage came on board, and in a short time the owner of the baggage, who was a female, appeared.

My crew consisted of one white steersman, one colored steersman, two white drivers, one colored bowman, and one colored female cook. When the lady arrived I stood aboard of the stern deck and assisted her aboard. When she went down into the cabin and saw the colored cook, she was taken completely by surprise. The colored steersman just then happened to go down into the cabin after something. The lady was sitting on the locker, and when she saw the colored steersman she went immediately to the other side of the boat. After the bowman had got his lines snugly curled, he went down into the cabin, and she accosted him, saying that she would like to see the captain. Accordingly, I was called, and went down to see what she wanted. The light shone in my face so that she could easily see my features. The lady, after seeing me, suddenly sprang to her feet, and with great shortness of breath exclaimed, "Well, I never! well, I never! well, I never." I made a bow and left her, and ordered the cook to set her state-room doors open, and to take off all the bedding from the middle berth, and supply clean bedding from the locker, so that she might see that the bedding was changed, and I requested the cook to tell the surprised lady to take the middle berth. She refused to go to bed, and sat up all night.

We arrived at Lock 21, north end of the Akron locks, at midnight. At nearly every lock there was a house or grocery, and I instructed the crew to keep the blinds on the boat closed, so that the lady should not know she was in a village; for, seeing that she was afraid of colored people, I wanted to give her full opportunity of getting acquainted with them before she arrived at her home in Circleville. We arrived at Lock 1 a little after daylight; that brought us on the Wolf Creek level. On going into the Wolf Creek lock, seeing that the lock was ready, we ran the boat right into the lock, and the hands divided, a part on one side of the boat, and a part on the other side. I gave the driver the signal, and he opened the wicket, lowered the boat down, and the lady was prevented from getting off there, if she had felt disposed to do so. When we came to the Fulton lock we pursued the same course as at the former lock. Before we had got to this point, and while we were yet on the Wolf Creek level, I invited the lady to breakfast, which she refused, saying that she did not feel very well. When we arrived at the

Fulton Lock, it brought us to the Massillon level, and it being dinner time, I invited the lady to dinner. She still complained of not feeling very well, but took a piece of pie from where she stood. Then we arrived at the Bethlehem level, and when tea was ready, I invited her to tea, and she took a cup of tea and a biscuit.

Just about this time we passed through a strip of woods about a mile in length. The moon was full, and it was a beautiful evening. The cook, having got through with her cabin work, came on deck. While she was proceeding towards the deck, the lady passenger followed her in a hesitating manner. They promenaded the deck together for a while, and then retired. I suppose the lady took a good night's sleep, for I did not hear anything from her until the next morning. When breakfast was ready, on receiving an invitation, she readily took a seat at the table, and ate a hearty meal, and from that time on she felt reconciled to her surroundings, and conversed freely with the cook and all on board. When we arrived at Circleville she left us. I provided means for the conveyance of her baggage, and on her leaving she thanked me, and said, "Captain, when I first came aboard your boat, not being "accustomed to travel in this way, I suppose I must "have acted quite awkward. Now, I must return my "thanks to you and your crew, for the kind treatment I "have received. I never traveled so comfortably in all "my life, and I expect to go north soon, and I will defer "my journey until you are going north, even if I am "obliged to wait two or three days." I never saw the lady again after that.

CHAPTER VI.

Prior to the time that I was engaged as captain on the canal boat as narrated, and during the time I was acting in the capacity of engineer for Mr. Hudson, I had taken considerable interest in the question of the education of the colored children. About the year 1832 I called a meeting of the colored men of Cleveland, and among others John Brown, Alexander Bowman, and David Smith. Mr. John H. Hudson gave us the use of a room on the mill premises to keep school in for colored children, and at that meeting we hired a half breed to teach the children, paying him $20 a month, and he taught for us three months; when he left we hired a young lady by the name of Clarissa Wright as teacher. Her parents lived in Talmadge, Ohio, and she taught about two months and a-half, when, in consequence of her mother's sickness, she had to leave. Then we employed a man by the name of M. M. Clark, from the East. I don't think he taught over three months. While he was teaching I called a meeting of colored men and suggested to them the propriety of calling a State convention of colored men, which was done, and, as far as I know, it was the first colored convention ever known in the United States; at least I never had heard of one before. After having agreed upon calling the convention we proposed for that purpose to employ Mr. Clark, our then school teacher, to canvass the State, and lecture to the colored people on the propriety of calling a State convention. He done so, and the State convention in 1835 was called in the City of Columbus as a consequence of our effort, and that convention organized itself into what was then called "the School Fund

Society." The business and object of that was to establish schools in different parts of the State for colored children. We established one in Cincinnati, one in Columbus, one in Springfield, and another in Cleveland, and that convention decided to employ M. M. Clark as an agent to raise funds for the support of the schools. The first donation was by James S. Clark, Esq., and in canvassing the State the good citizens of the State responded to the call. We kept these schools going for about two years, and several of the adult colored people of Cleveland, not having had the benefits of education before extended to them, went to the schools established in Cleveland, and learned to read and write pretty well. A gentleman, whose name I do not now remember, but who lived in the southern part of the State, donated for the support of these schools a tract of twenty-five acres.

I was not satisfied, however, as long as the black laws remained on the statute books, which prohibited colored children from going to the public schools, and being anxious for their repeal, in common with many of the colored people of the State I called another meeting of the colored people of Cleveland, and suggested the propriety of circulating a petition to be sent to the Legislature for the repeal of those odious laws, and I also proposed that we employ some lecturers to lecture through the State and raise a sentiment in favor of the repeal of those laws. We accordingly employed John L. Watson, of Cleveland, William H. Day, of Oberlin, and R. R. Chancellor, of Chillicothe, for that purpose, and shortly after they were employed they obtained permission to lecture in the State House at Columbus, and we found good results ensued from the lectures. I don't exactly remember the year, but I think it was in 1841. The Legislature was then Democratic, and

Hon. Franklin T. Backus was elected to the Legislature, and it was through his efforts in our behalf, and the effect those lectures had on the people that the black laws were repealed, with the exception of the school law prohibiting colored children from going to the public schools.

About the year 1843 a couple of slaves ran away from Tennessee, and were recommended here to one Henry Jackson, a barber, who was reputed to be an abolitionist, and they stayed here under his protection from four to six weeks. During that time he learned where they were from, and the names of their owners. A reward having been offered for their apprehension, Jackson communicated that fact to H. V. Wilson, who afterwards became Judge of the U. S. District Court in Cleveland. Jackson could not write, but he engaged Mr. Wilson to open a correspondence with the owners of the two men. At least I concluded, from the fact that Jackson could not write, and all the circumstances, that Mr. Wilson did the writing.

After the fugitives had been in Cleveland about six weeks they left and went to Buffalo, and shortly after the agent of the owners arrived in Cleveland. Learning from Jackson that the boys were in Buffalo there was a consultation held between Mr. Wilson, Jackson and the agent, and it was concluded to get the men back to Cleveland, or in Ohio, for the reason that colored men were allowed to testify in the State of New York, but could not testify in Ohio. The black laws had not yet been repealed. They planned that Jackson, the agent, and Mr. Wilson, should go to Buffalo, and that Jackson should be their spokesman. The names of the two boys were Alexander Williams and John Houston. Before they went to Buffalo, Williams applied to J. F. Hanks, who was a portrait painter, to become an apprentice, but

Hanks did not employ him, and Jackson, as spokesman
for the trio, on their arrival in Buffalo, represented to
Williams that Mr. Hanks had agreed to employ him as
apprentice, and had sent him down to see him (Williams,) to have him come back to Cleveland and enter
into the apprenticeship, and he represented to John
Houston, who was formerly a cook in the South, that
there was a new brig just launched in Cleveland, and
the Captain had employed him to engage a cook, and so
he had come to Buffalo to have him ship on board of
the new brig as cook.

Before leaving Cleveland for Buffalo there had been a
warrant issued and placed in the hands of Madison
Miller, who was Sheriff, that was to be served on the
boys as soon as they landed in Cleveland. By reason of
the representations thus made to the boys they were
induced to return to Cleveland. They no sooner landed
than they were arrested and placed in jail. A crowd of
colored people, myself among the number, gathered
around the jail late, in order to see that they were not
run off during the night without a chance of hearing.
Charles Stetson, Esq., kindly volunteered his services
gratis as attorney for the boys, and we employed to
assist him Thomas Bolton, Esq., who was a Democrat.
We paid Mr. Bolton $25 to take the case. The agent,
Mr. Lindenberger, employed H. B. Payne, Esq., and
Hon. Horace Foote, and so the boys, in a day or two,
were brought before Judge Barber, (not the present
Judge Barber.)

When the boys were brought out and it was ascertained how they were deceived and brought back from
Buffalo, Edward Wade, Esq., interposed a motion to
the court asking for a continuance of the cause for
twelve days. It was the law that when a fugitive slave
was arrested and put in jail or custody, that if he could

furnish bail of $1,000, he would be released from prison until the expiration of the time of adjournment. So Alexander Bowman, John Brown and myself furnished the required bail. Then I took the boy Alexander Williams from the jail and went with him to Buffalo by the advice of the lawyers, to ascertain the particulars in the case. I had a letter from Mr. Bolton, directed to George A. Barker, Esq., the Prosecuting Attorney at Buffalo. I arrived in Buffalo about six o'clock in the evening. Mr. H. B. Payne took passage on the same boat and was on his way to New York. I went to Mr. Barker's office and presented the letter. Mr. Barker informed me that on the same boat I came down on in the mail there was a letter from H. B. Payne. He read it to me, and it was in substance, if not the precise words, as follows:

"George A. Barker, Esq.:

" There were two runaway negroes taken up in Cleveland (naming the day), much to the satisfaction of all the citizens of Cleveland, except a few black abolitionists and a few white negroes. I expect to go to New York in a day or two, and defer action until I see you."

Mr. Barker then said to me: " I am well acquainted with Thomas Bolton, a brother Democrat." So that night he had a jury called, and Alexander Williams was called in before the jury and testified as to the manner in which they were decoyed. The jury decided that these men were kidnapped, and Mr. Barker that same night wrote a letter to the Governor of New York for a requisition on the Governor of Ohio for the men that kidnapped the boys, and Mr. Barker requested me to call at his office the next morning at 8 o'clock. I came to his office at the appointed time, and had not been there over ten minutes, when who should come in but Mr. H. B. Payne. Mr. Payne and I did not say much

to each other. He appeared a little confused to see me.
Mr. Barker handed me a letter to give to Mr. Bolton,
and so I returned that morning with Alexander Williams by steamer, and when we arrived in Cleveland I
delivered the prisoner to the authorities, and he was
returned back to jail. A day or two after the requisition was forwarded to the Governor of Ohio for the
arrest of Jackson, the agent of Lindenberger, and H.
V. Wilson, to answer the charge as found by the jury
for kidnapping. The officer in charge of the requisition went to Columbus and presented his papers to
the Governor, who issued a warrant for the arrest of
the persons named. Jackson, having heard of this, ran
away, as also did Lindenberger, so that when the day of
trial of the boys came they were not present. The trial,
however, had not come off, and one day, as I happened
to go to a meeting, on my return about half past nine
in the evening there was a rap at my door, and when I
opened it, I found to my surprise Alexander Williams.
I hardly knew what to do with Williams. My home
was then on the corner of Bond and York, (now Hamilton) street, which was then in the woods. I dared not
harbor him in my house, so I took him to the woods
five or six rods off and had him climb a tree till I could
find a place of safety. One Deacon Hamlin was building a one-story brick house on Prospect street, which
was enclosed but not finished. I got some comforters
and Buffalo robes, and placed them in the building, and
then I went back to the woods after Williams, but I
had lost track of the tree he was in, and wandered
about, afraid to call, lest I should be heard by some one.
After considerable search I found the tree, had him
come down, and took him to the building, and kept him
there for several days. His complexion was a bright
mulatto. I made a composition, and painted all the

visible parts of the man, and made a very black man of him, so he walked about the streets of Cleveland boldly and no one recognized him as Alexander Williams. He afterwards left Cleveland for New York State, and, perhaps, went into Canada. On the day of trial the other boy, John Houston, was brought into Court, but Jackson and Lindenberger not being at the trial, there was no one to appear against the boy, and he was discharged.

CHAPTER VII.

The establishment of colored schools in Ohio, in which I had taken an active part as already stated, made a decided improvement in the condition of the colored people, but like other people who have not had the benefits of education, there were many among them who were not from the force of circumstances over honest. Reform of course was needed, and I undertook in every way possible to do whatever I could towards improvement and advancement of my people in this respect. Very often, when charges were brought against colored men, I would go their bail, in order that they might have a fair opportunity to prepare for trial and test the truth of the charge, and being a property owner, I was called upon in many cases for bail, which I seldom refused. On one occasion, when Hon. Samuel Starkweather was Judge of the Court of Common Pleas, a colored man by the name of Archie Lorton was arrested for horse stealing, and I went his bail. Shortly after I bailed him, he packed up his things and ran away to Canada. As soon as I ascertained where he was, I employed Deputy Sheriff S. P. Bosworth to go with me to Canada and arrest and bring him back. We went to Detroit and crossed over into Windsor, and thence proceeded to London, where I got track of him. I found that he was at a little town called Waterford, twelve miles west of London. We proceeded to a magistrate in London in order to procure a warrant for his arrest. The magistrate claimed that he had no jurisdiction in the matter, and referred me to another magistrate, who again referred me to what they called the high magistrate. I went to the high magistrate, and he also refused to issue a warrant, for the reason that he had no jurisdiction in the matter. I then went and employed a lawyer, and the lawyer went with me to the high magistrate and demanded a warrant; and after convincing the magistrate that he was justified in issuing a warrant, it was granted. We then proceeded to Waterford and arrested Lorton a little after dark, and then put up at the American Hotel. The Bailiff left the prisoner in my charge, and I kept watch over him all night, and the next morning the Bailiff took him out of my hands and placed him in jail, and reported to the Mayor of the city, who ordered the prisoner to be brought before him on Monday morning at 9 o'clock. On our way to the Mayor's office he shouted that he was a slave, and that we were kidnappers, and were taking him back into slavery. In a few minutes we were surrounded by forty or fifty infuriated colored men, and we expected every moment that they would mob us. The deputy undertook to pacify them, but they would not listen to him, and at length I succeeded in getting them to hear me. I told them how the matter was, and they believed my statement, and some of them exclaimed that if he was a horse thief they did not want him there, and were glad to see him removed.

Lorton, having left this wife in Waterford, he then and there agreed that if we would go back to Waterford and meet his wife, that he would go with us to Port Stanley without a hearing. We consented to do this and started toward Waterford, and on the way we met the stage coming towards London with the prisoner's wife. We stopped the stage, and upon her statement that she had left something behind, and that she must go back to Waterford, I agreed to take her place in the stage, and that she should take my place in the carriage with the bailiff. They were to proceed on to Waterford, and the prisoner promised if that was done he would go back to the United States without insisting on a trial in Canada.

I took her place in the stage accordingly, and took charge of her baggage, which I checked to Detroit. I agreed to take the railroad and meet the party at Lobi Station, the first station after leaving London for Windsor. I met them at Lobi Station as agreed on, and then the prisoner refused to accompany us to the United States, which I had in part anticipated. Then we had to go back to London, and after we arrived there, the Mayor ordered him to be put in jail till I could get a requisition, limiting the time to three weeks. I then went home, and proceeded at once to Columbus and called on Governor Medill. He said that he had no jurisdiction outside of the United States, and therefore could not grant a requisition, but referred me to the Secretary of State—Samuel Williamson, Esq., who was then Prosecuting Attorney in Cleveland, at my request, wrote a letter to the Secretary of State, and the reply of the Secretary of State was, that horse stealing was grand larceny, and did not come within the category of the Ashburton Treaty, and that he had no jurisdiction to issue a requisition in the matter. I was therefore left without any remedy, and had been put to great expense in attempting to bring Lorton back.

Some time afterwards, Lorton committed some depredation in Canada and fled to Adrian, Michigan, and as soon as I heard of his being there, I got the necessary requisition from the Governor, and had him arrested and brought to Cleveland. He was tried, convicted, and sent to the penitentiary for seven years.

CHAPTER VIII.

I will state a circumstance that may perhaps be of some interest, that occurred shortly before the war: A young colored girl ran away from Wheeling, Va., and came to Cleveland, and took up her residence in the family of Mr. W. E. Ambush. After she remained there a short period of time, it was ascertained by her owners as to her whereabouts, and they came to Cleveland in search of her. The girl went by the name of Lucy, and she had sought employment in the family of George A. Benedict, and she left Ambush and went to Benedict's. As soon as her owners, who were father and son, named Goshorn, arrived in Cleveland, they obtained a warrant for the girl's arrest, which was placed in the hands of Seth A. Abbey, then United States Marshal, and she was arrested by him and placed in the county jail. A number of the citizens of Cleveland immediately employed Hon. R. P. Spalding on behalf of the girl, and she was taken out of the custody of the Marshal, on a writ of *habeas corpus* issued by Judge Tilden, Probate Judge of Cuyahoga County. When they were ready for hearing, Judge Tilden inquired of Mr. Spalding whether he desired the prisoner to be brought into his court. Judge Spalding replied that the investigation could proceed without her presence. Thereupon, after a hearing had, Judge Tilden remanded her back again into the custody of the Marshal, who kept her in jail.

She was brought before Judge Wilson, U. S. District Judge. On her way to the Court a crowd of people had gathered near the Post-office building, in which the Court was held, and there was a great deal of excitement about the girl. One of the men in the crowd approached a colored man by the name of C. M. Richardson, who had been a resident of Cleveland for a number of years, and dealt Mr. Richardson a stunning blow on the head, which felled him to the ground. The man evidently thought that Mr. Richardson was there for the purpose of rescuing the girl. Another man in the crowd, an Irishman, stepped up to a colored man by the name of Munson, and raised a club and was about to strike him, when Hon. Jabez M. Fitch, who happened to be near, interposed, and prevented the threatened blow.

The girl was brought into the U. S. Court room, and before the hearing commenced, Mr. Ambush had some words with young Goshorn, right in the Court room, and pistols were drawn on both sides, but they were prevented from firing by the interposition of people in the Court room. After the trial the Judge ordered the girl to be delivered up to her master, who took her back with him to Wheeling, where she was placed in jail and severely punished.

One of the arguments among the people generally, why the girl should be given up was, that it might prevent rebellion on the part of the South, which perhaps is an indication of the sentiment then prevailing. The war, however, was sure to come, and was not the result of any wrangling over a captive female, as some of the wars we read of in history, but was founded upon sterner and nobler principles. Not the fate of a single individual, but of a whole race, was involved in the great struggle which afterwards burst forth, and opened the flood-gates of liberty.

When the Union Army arrived in Wheeling, the girl was liberated, and her master, Mr. Goshorn, who had become a prisoner of war, was incarcerated in the same jail in which he had confined Lucy.

On the breaking out of the rebellion in 1861, the condition of the colored people was such, that not having the privilege of universal suffrage, they had not the opportunity to exercise a very wide or extended influence upon the living question which then agitated the country, and, as a consequence, they were left almost powerless to organize or do anything in co-operation with the white people towards the suppression of the rebellion, or towards the emancipation of their race. Nevertheless, there were a great many white citizens who were deeply in sympathy with the colored race.

On the election of Mr. Lincoln as President, the Republican party made very rapid strides towards its present strength and unity, and many of the citizens of Cleveland, among whom I might mention Hon. D. K. Tilden, John Huntington, Wm. P. Fogg, Hon. Sherlock J. Andrews, Hon. R. F. Payne, Charles Stetson, Esq., John A. Foot, Esq., J. M. Hoyt, Esq., Edward Wade, Esq., George A. Benedict, Edwin Cowles, Rev. Dr. Aiken, Rev. Levi Tucker, M. C. Younglove, Richard C. Parsons, and many others, were active Republicans at the time, and took an earnest part in all the deliberations of the Republican party.

Whenever the colored people made any movement, or needed any advice, they consulted with these respective gentlemen. The Rev. Dr. Aiken especially, interested himself in behalf of the condition of the colored people. Long before, when the fugitive slave law was being passed, at a meeting held at the First Presbyterian Church, of which he was the pastor, he strongly denounced that law, and expressed sentiments in favor of resisting its enforcement. At that meeting it was resolved, that in case of the arrest of a fugitive slave,

the church bells of the city should be rung as notice to
the people of the arrest. Mr. M. C. Younglove offered
a reward of five dollars to the sexton who should on
such an occasion ring the first bell. Rev. Dr. Aiken
afterwards proved to be a powerful friend to the colored people, and aided them by his counsel in their
deliberations.

When the rebellion first broke out, I undertook to
have a meeting called of the colored people of Cleveland, and, in conjunction with others, a meeting was
called at the National Hall, on the Public Square. It
was proposed at that meeting that the colored people of
Cleveland should organize military companies to assist
in putting down the rebellion, and it was also proposed
that an application should be made to the Governor for
that purpose. But when the committee delegated for
that purpose laid our request before the Governor, he
declined to accept it, giving as a reason, that the matter
was in the hands of the white people, and that they
would take care of it. When Governor Brough was
elected, a similar meeting was called, and another application for the same purpose was made to Governor
Brough, but with no better result. In some of the New
England States however, they had permitted colored
companies to be formed, and many of the colored men
of Cleveland left Ohio and went to Massachusetts, and
joined colored regiments there formed, among others,
Wm. Underhill, John Brown and Charles Brown, sons
of John Brown, (otherwise known as John Brown, the
barber,) Joseph Richardson and Benjamin Richardson,
and others. Shortly afterwards the proclamation of
emancipation was issued, and then it was that colored
companies began to organize in Ohio, and from that
time on, the influence of the colored people became
more powerful. The resistance at that time of the

leading copperheads was very bitter, and a strong aversion and repugnance was manifested by many of them against the colored people taking part in public affairs. The prejudice then existing, and which I suppose existed in every similar instance in history, where a people who have been looked upon as a despised race, and have risen above the condition in which they have been placed by unfortunate circumstances, has pretty well worn away in the Northern States, and it is not strange to see a colored man propose measures in common with his white fellow-citizens for the common weal and benefit of all. Distinctions which are founded on human policy, without reference to the divine or natural law, and which tend to the degradation of a set of human beings, cannot be lasting, and must sooner or later succumb to the dictates of reason and humanity. Would this were accomplished in the Southern States. There intimidation and threats make the life of the colored man a thousand times more miserable than the worst condition of bondage. But as right will sooner or later prevail, the day will come when another nemesis will overtake and destroy the evil at the South.

It has been demonstrated that an intelligent colored man can be as good a citizen as an intelligent white man, and the same reasoning will hold good between an ignorant colored man and an ignorant white man.

I am now eighty-three years of age, and I thank God that he has spared my life long enough to witness the change wrought in the condition of the colored people. We read of the miraculous deliverance of the Israelites from bondage. It seems hardly less than a miracle that has been the means of unloosening the shackles of the colored man. I firmly believe it to be the interposition of Divine Providence wrought through the instrumentality of the Republican party.

In conclusion, I can only say as did Simeon of old, when he saw the promised Messiah, " Now, Lord, let- "test thou thy servant depart in peace according to thy " Word, for mine eyes have seen thy salvation."